Panda Power

To Darling Kirane
Have a wonderful
Christmas —
Lots of Love
Archie

ℛ
RAVETTE PUBLISHING

The mission of WWF - the global environment network - is to stop
the degradation of the planet's natural environment
and to build a future in which humans live in harmony with nature.

For further information check out the website www.wwf-uk.org

WWF. Taking action for a living planet.

Panda Patrol © 2001 Tandem Licensing & Media Ltd. and WWF-UK
Panda symbol © 1986 WWF Panda word ® WWF registered trademark
WWF-UK registered charity number 1081247

Created by Frank Bell & Colin Bowler

Written by Frank Bell

Illustrated by Paul Seaman

Printed on 100% recycled post consumer waste

First published by Ravette Publishing 2002

Ravette Publishing Limited,

Unit 3, Tristar Centre,
Star Road, Partridge Green, West Sussex RH13 8RA

ISBN: 1 84161 084 4

Monti and the gang were enjoying a lazy
morning in Panda Valley, when suddenly, their
friend Ozzie, the Australian zoologist, appeared.

"G'day Panda Patrol!" he cried.

The family jumped up and ran to greet him.

Ozzie asked the family to fly their magic carpet to the coast and help him find a way to stop dolphins getting caught in fishermen's nets.

"What are we waiting for?" asked Ma Jong, and before you could say 'Panda Patrol', the magic carpet was flying across Panda Valley.

As soon as they arrived at the coast, Monti launched the Panda Patrol raft and Slip Slap Slop loaded on his surfboard.

The wind was very strong and they were soon far out to sea.

Monti let out a yell and pointed to the dolphins leaping in the distance.

Slip Slap Slop launched his surfboard and sped off to meet the dolphins.

They greeted him with leaps and somersaults as they filled the air with their excited clicking noises.

By the time the others arrived, Slip Slap Slop had come up with the clever idea of the 'Panda Pinga'.

The 'Panda Pinga' would fit onto the top of the fishing nets and send out a powerful radio signal to warn the dolphins to stay away from the nets.

Everyone thought this was a great idea, especially the dolphins.

They decided to head back to the beach and start making 'Panda Pingas' for the fishermen's nets.

The dolphins decided that it would be great fun to give the raft a huge shove down the biggest wave they could find.

Slip Slap Slop started to paddle towards the clicking sound.

Head down, lying flat on his tummy, his arms churned furiously through the foamy water.

Four strong dolphins lined up to push the raft through the water while Slip Slap Slop and two dolphins watched out for a huge wave.

Suddenly, one of the dolphins started to click excitedly.

Then, the second dolphin started clicking wildly.

This confused Slip Slap Slop who stopped paddling and stood up on his surfboard to see what all the fuss was about.

What he saw made his tummy feel empty and his legs turn to jelly.

Slip Slap Slop's surfboard was wobbling at the top of the biggest wave he had ever seen! Suddenly, the wave started to curl over.

Slip Slap Slop tried very hard to keep his balance ... but he couldn't!

His foot slipped, he fell forward and banged his head on the board before he tumbled down the wave.

A dolphin at the bottom of the wave saw him fall and let out a warning, clicking to the other dolphins, who sped to his rescue.

Slip Slap Slop was taken back to the raft on the back of the dolphin who had rescued him.

"From now on, I think I'll leave surfing to the coolest surfers in the ocean."

"Who's that?" clicked the dolphins.

"You, of course!" smiled Slip Slap Slop.